Little Black Car

IMANI DIOP

Copyright © 2021 Imani Diop
All rights reserved
First Edition

PAGE PUBLISHING, INC.
Conneaut Lake, PA

First originally published by Page Publishing 2021

ISBN 978-1-6624-2127-3 (pbk)
ISBN 978-1-6624-2128-0 (digital)

Printed in the United States of America

*This is for being the engine that keeps me going,
For the motivation you gave me the
day you took your first breath,
Strong willed about your desires,
The animated old soul that makes me smile,
Comfortable in your own skin,
Who would have known the parent
would learn from the child!
To my Xavier
(currently age five)*

Little black car realizes after several failed attempts to be like others that the best way to make friends is to be himself (for ages two to seven).

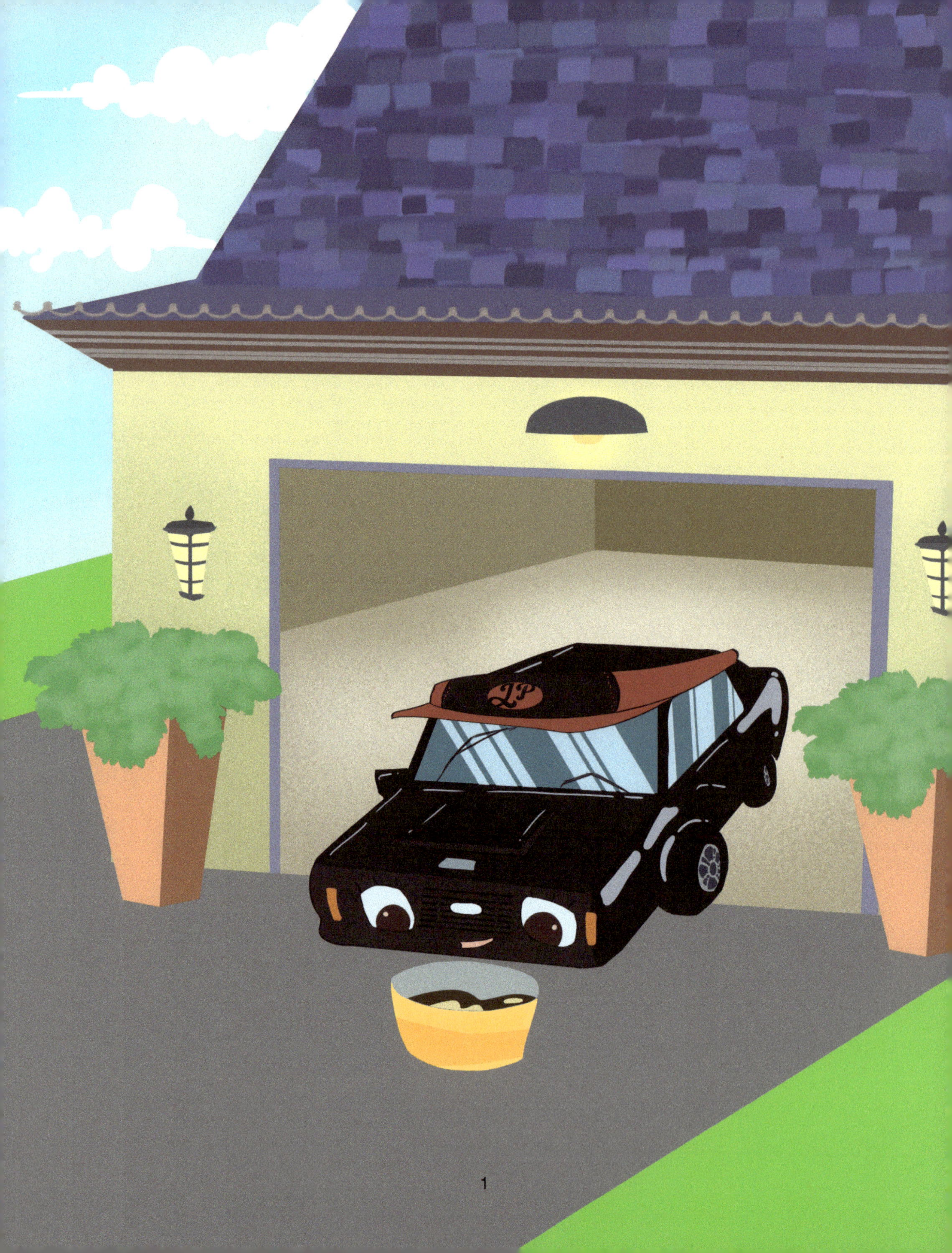

It's a great day to race! The sun is shining bright, and the lanes are dry, Little Black Car thought as he looked outside the window. He drove to the garage to get a drink. *Gulp, gulp, gulp, haaa!* Little Black Car let out a huge sigh after guzzling down five gallons of petrol.

"Mom says if I drink my petrol, I'll be superfast."

Vroom, vroom, vroom, he revved his engine. "I'm ready for racing!"

I wish I had a friend to race with me, Little Black Car thought, realizing he was the only car at the lanes.

Little Black Car drove across the street to see if he could find a friend to race with. He noticed Lightning leaving the car wash.

Then he thought, *If I do the wheelies my dad showed me, he will think that's cool, and then he will race with me.*

Little Black Car was so excited to show Lightning what he could do that he didn't notice the puddle of mud in front of him. He started ghost riding on two wheels like his dad showed him. Then he spun around and did three wheelies right in the mud. *Splat!*

"Hi, Lightning, do you remember me from school? I was wondering if you would like to race on the lanes with me? It's a perfect day for it!"

"Well, thanks, Black Car! No, I don't want to race. Now I have to go through the car wash all over again! You got mud all over me!" said Lightning in an angry tone.

"I'm so sorry, Lightning. I didn't mean to get you dirty," Black Car said as he drove away.

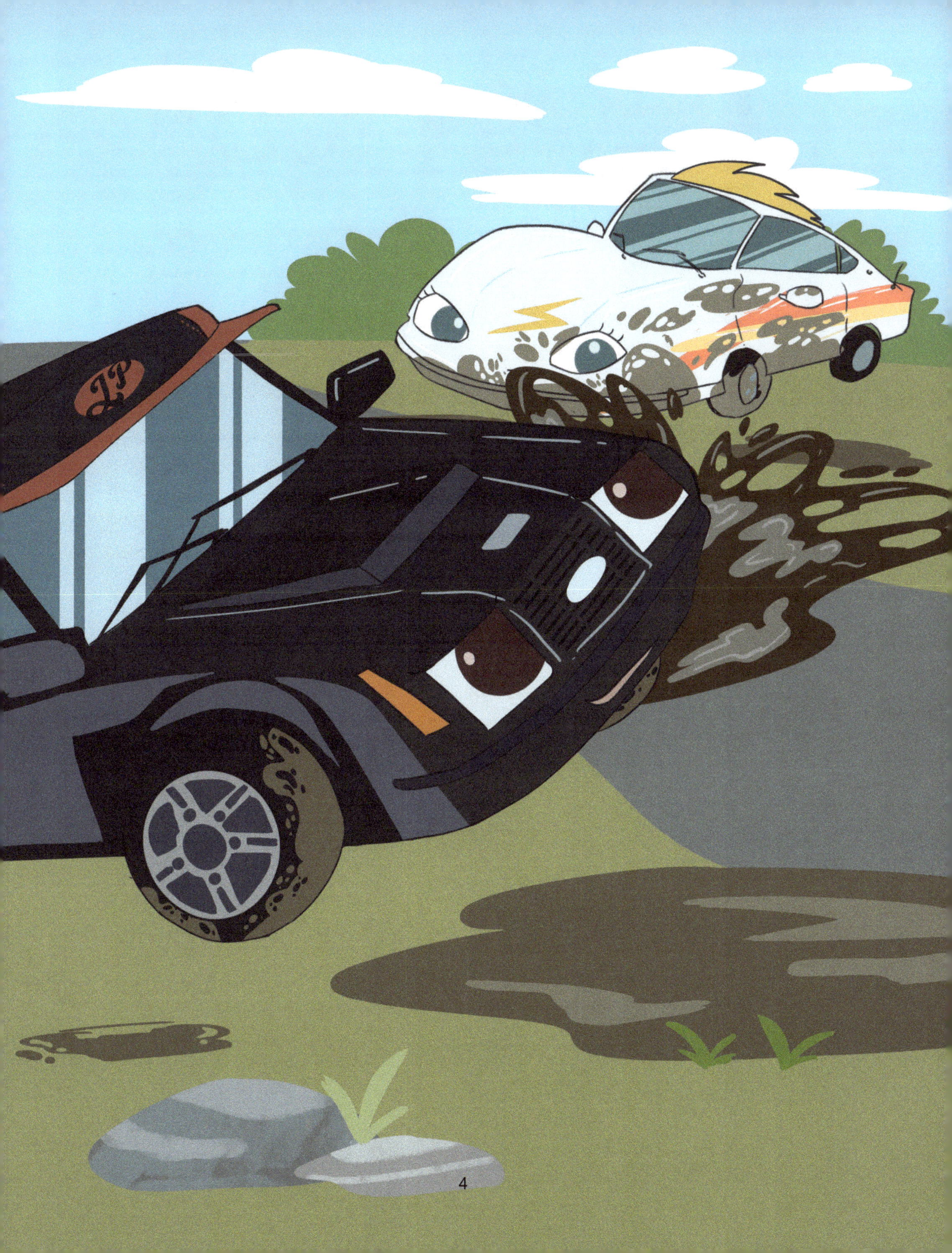

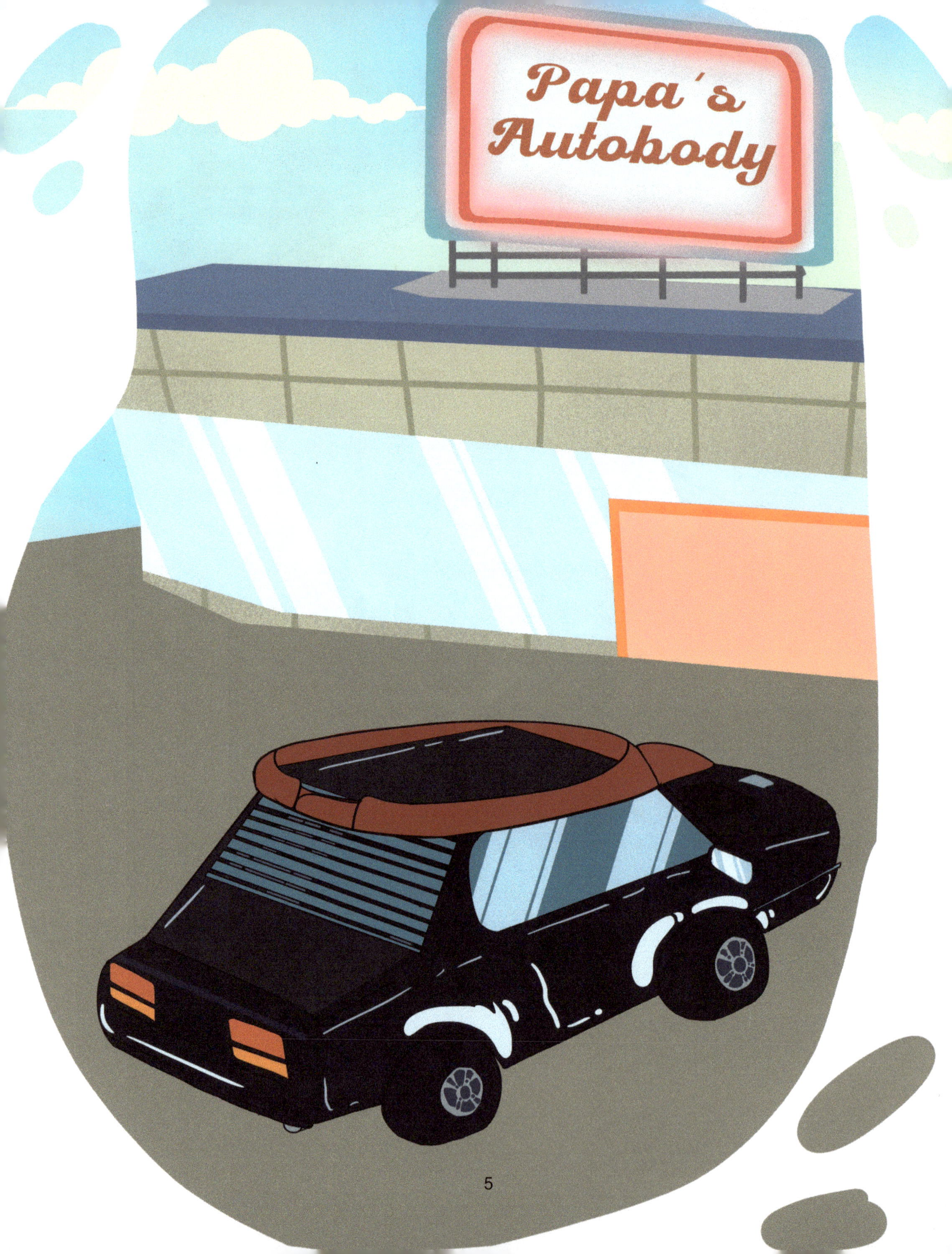
Papa's
Autobody

As Little Black Car drove on, he saw Speaker Box showing everyone his new speakers. "Aha, I have an idea! I bet if I had speakers like his, then they would think I look cool and want to race with me."

Vroom—Little Black Car drove to his dad's shop to put top-of-the-line speakers inside. "Dad, I want the loudest speakers you have."

Little Black Car raced back to the drive-in where he knew all the other cars would be.

Once he got close to his destination, he made an abrupt stop—*screech*. He turned his speakers up as loud as they would go.

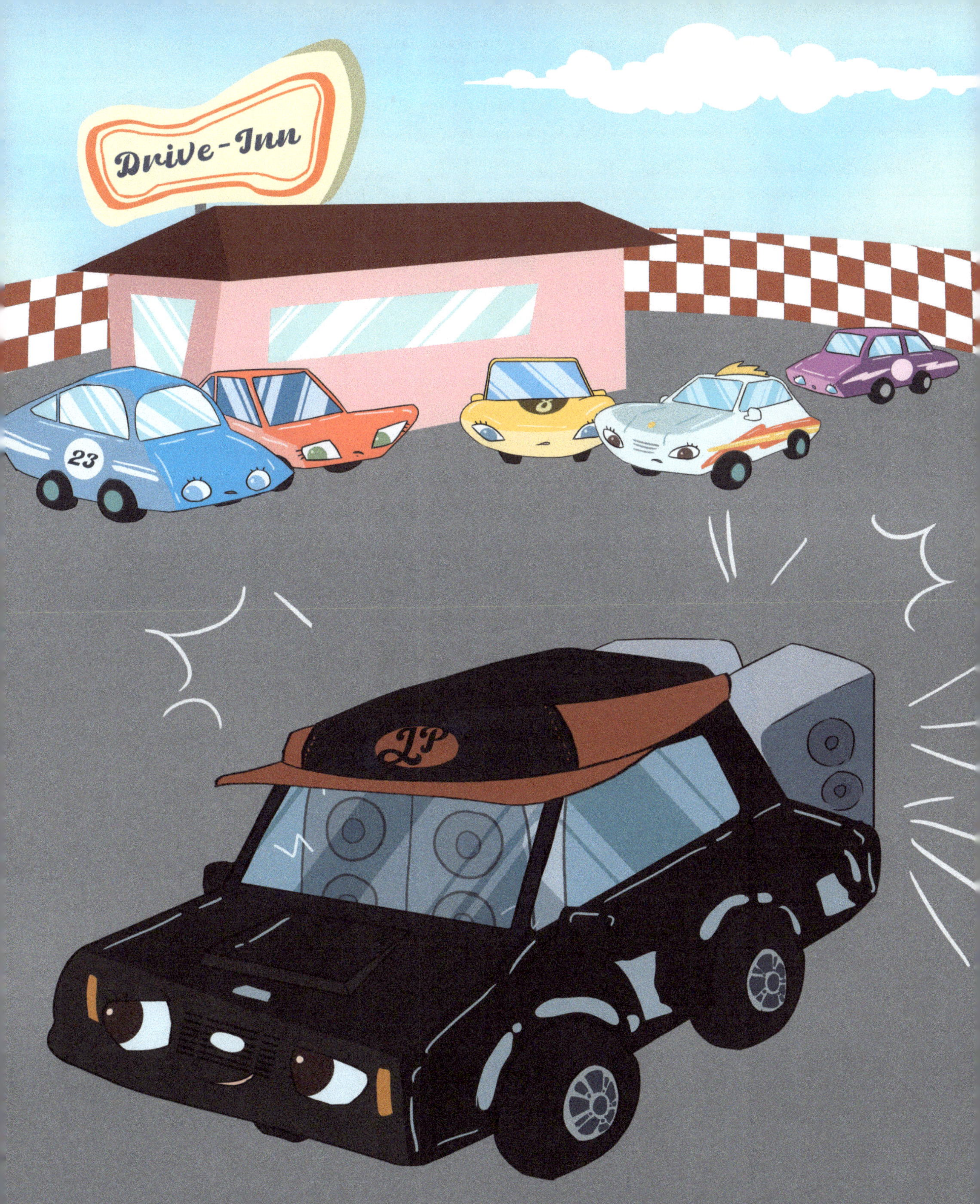
Drive-Inn
23
LP

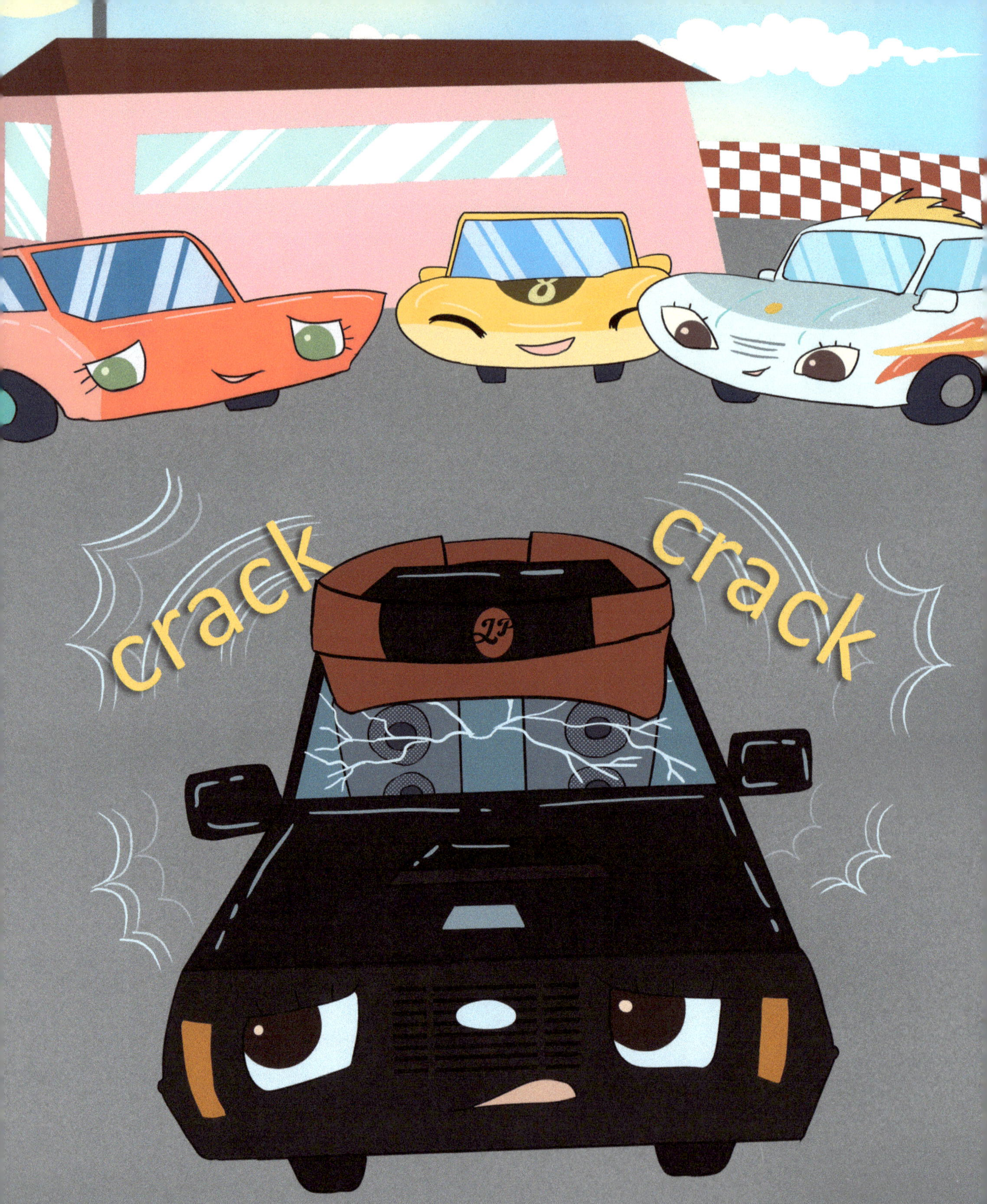
crack
crack

Boom, kaboom, the speakers played. "Hey, do you guys want to go to the lanes and race with me?"

No one heard Black Car. The music was so loud it hurt their ears. *Boom, kaboom, crack,* his speakers were so loud it cracked Little Black Car's windshield. All the other cars started laughing at Black Car. He was hurt by their reaction, and he drove away.

"Lightning didn't like my wheelies, and they laughed at my speakers." The sadness began to take over and then—

"Aha!" Suddenly he had an idea. "I bet if I had sparks and rims like some of the other cars from school, then they will race with me."

Vroom, vroom. Little Black Car drove back to his dad's body shop.

"Dad, I need a new paint job," he said while at the printer, printing the template. "Can you help me? I want sparks that you can see a mile away. Oh, and may I have a new set of rims please?" he asked while giving his dad a face he couldn't say no to.

Papa's Autobody

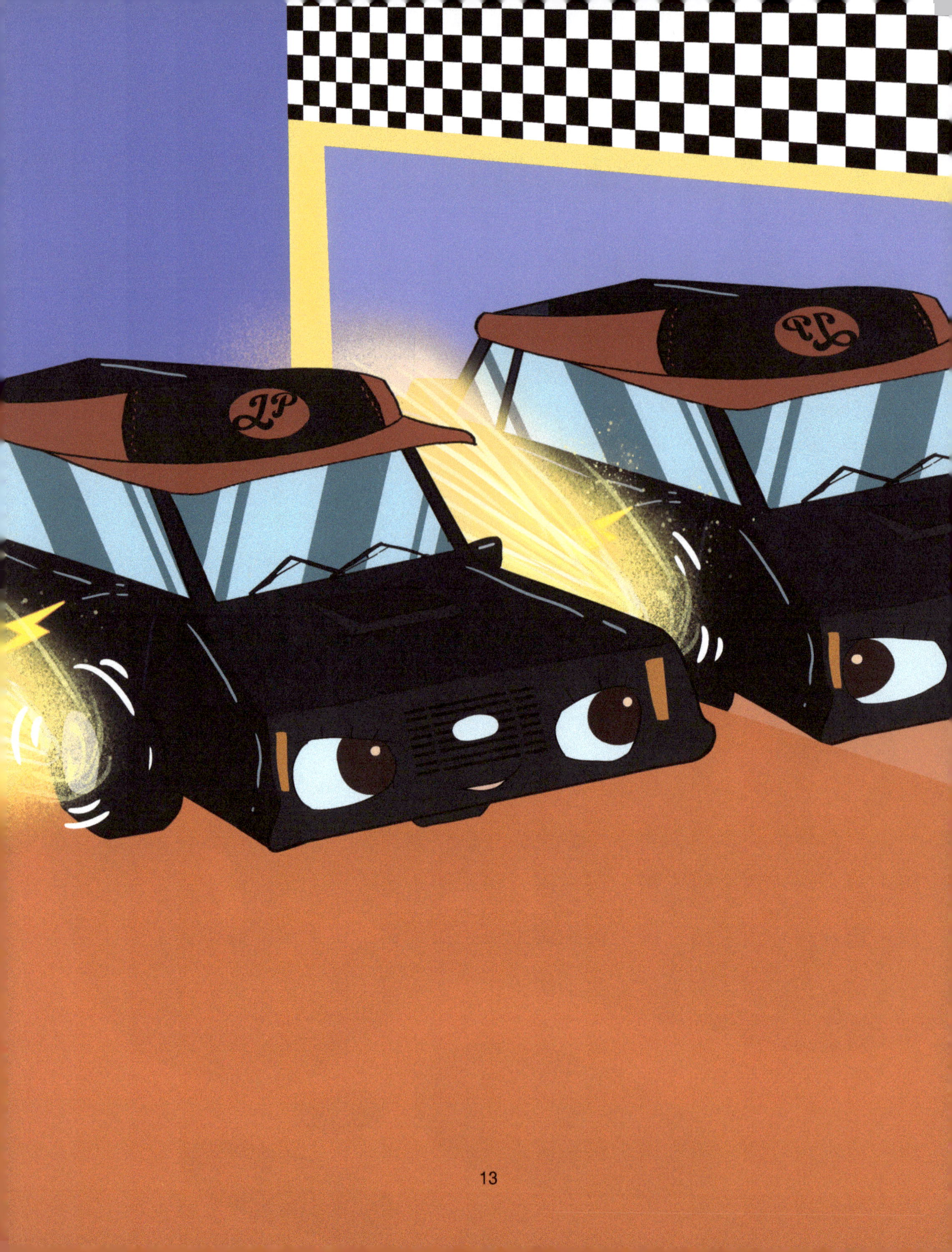

"*Chikaboom*, *chikaboom*, I look gooood! I can't wait to show everyone my new paint job. They are definitely going to race with me now."

Lightning and the gang were already at the fast lanes racing. *Zoom*—the reflection of two cars racing sped right past him.

"Awesome, can I race the winner next?"

The reflection from the sparks was blinding everyone. They drove backward to get away from the glare.

Little Black Car didn't realize they were driving backward so that they could see. He thought no one wanted to race with him, so he drove back to his dad's body shop.

fast lanes

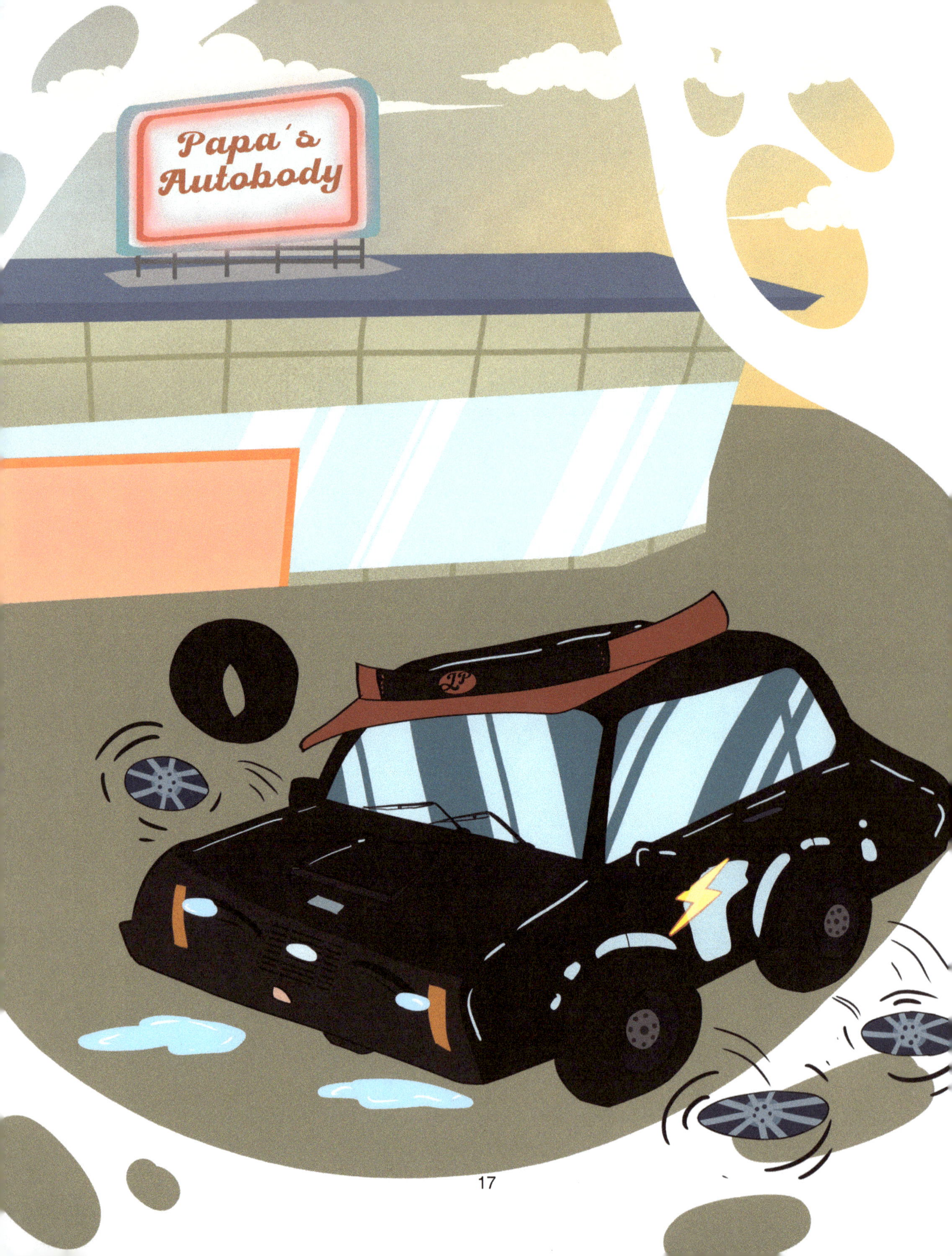
Papa's
Autobody

Little Black Car left feeling confused. All he wanted to do was race.

"Back so soon, son?" said Papa Car.

"I don't want these sparks anymore, or these rims." Little Black Car threw his new speakers on the floor—*bam!* "None of it made a difference anyway."

"Well, what do you mean it didn't make a difference?"

"I only wanted them to like me so we could race together. Lightning didn't like the cool tricks I learned from you. Instead, he got mad at me for getting mud on him. Everyone laughed at me when my windshield cracked from those loud speakers. And they drove away from me when I showed them my new paint job. It just isn't fair!"

"Hmmm, I see. Do you want to know the best way to make friends?"

"How? Please tell me, please!"

"Always be yourself! If they don't want to be your friend after that, it's their loss."

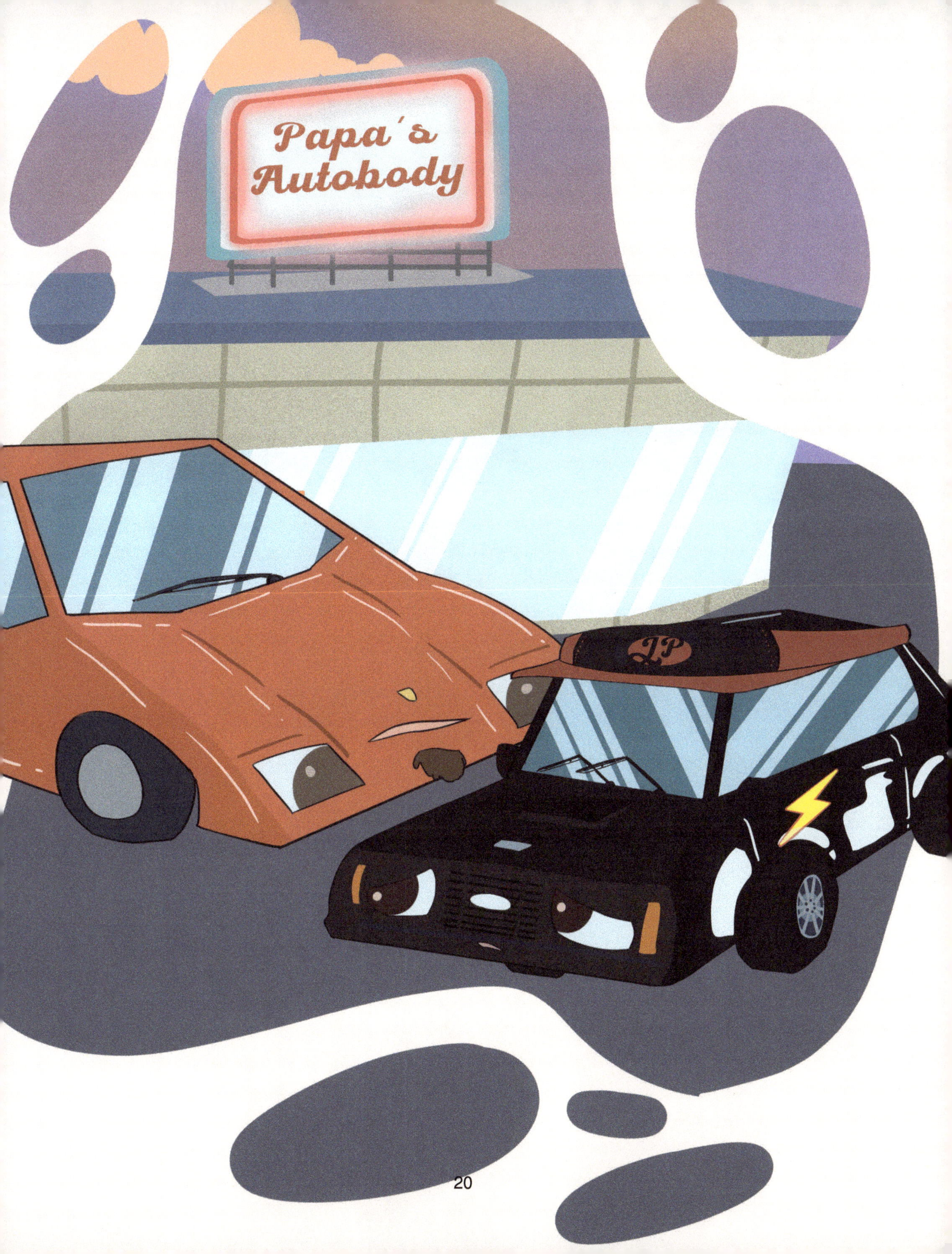
Papa's
Autobody

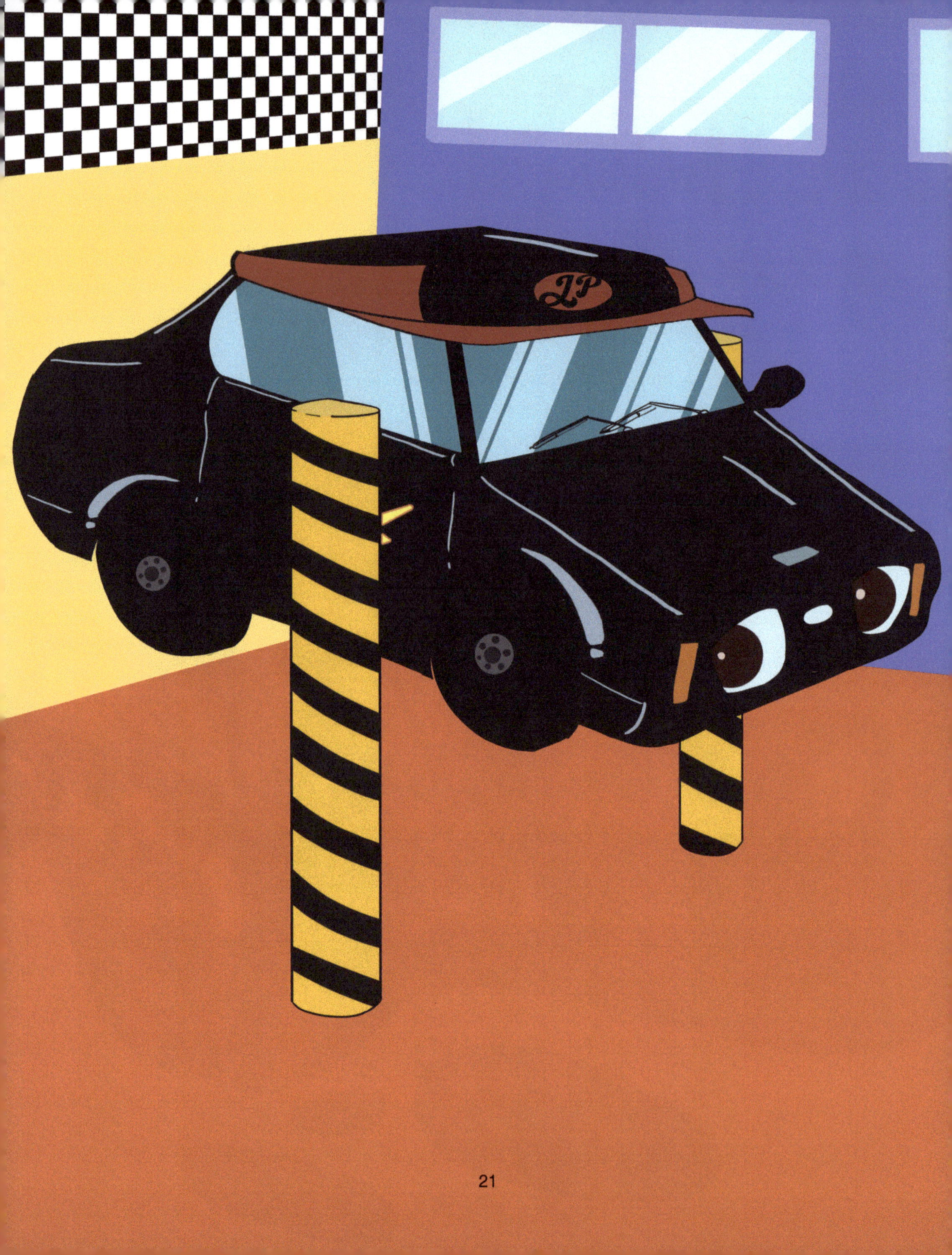

"I understand, Dad. Can you make me back how I was before? Just regular Little Black Car."

"You got it, my boy!"

Once he was done at his dad's shop, he drove back to the fast lanes.

"Hey, Little Black Car!" said Lightning. "Come over here. Do you like to race?"

"Are you kidding me? *Vroom, vroom*," he revved his engine. "I'm built for speed," said Little Black Car.

"You obviously haven't heard how lightning fast I am," said Lightning.

"Okay, boys, wheels on the starting line. "Ready!"

Vroom, vroom—you could hear Lightning and Little Black Car revving up for the race.

"Set!"

Both cars leaned forward. Both boys purred their engines with excitement. The light-pink sports car looked in her headlights to check her lip gloss.

"Go!" she said, releasing the flag.

Smoke filled the air as Little Black Car and Lighting began to race.

Fast La

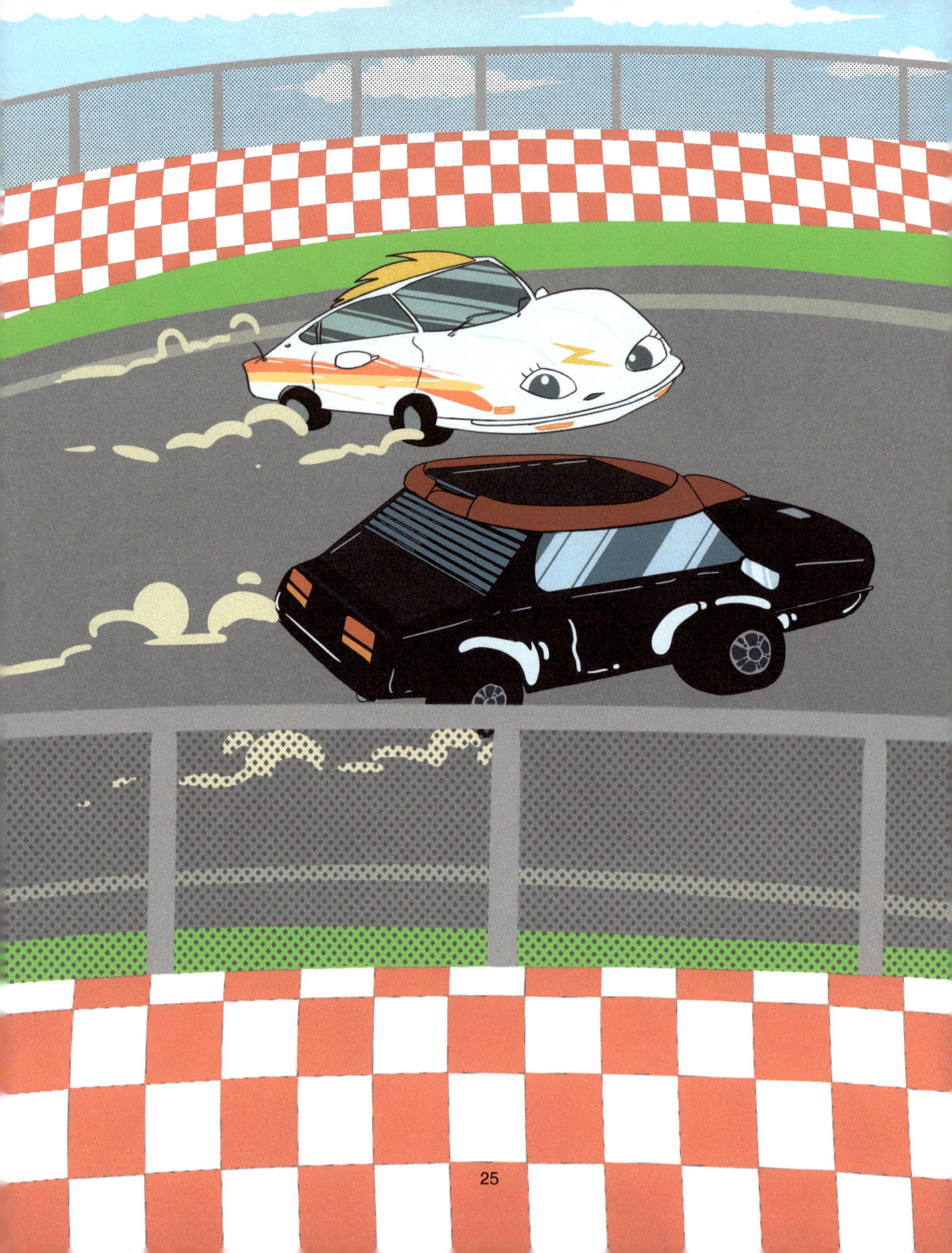

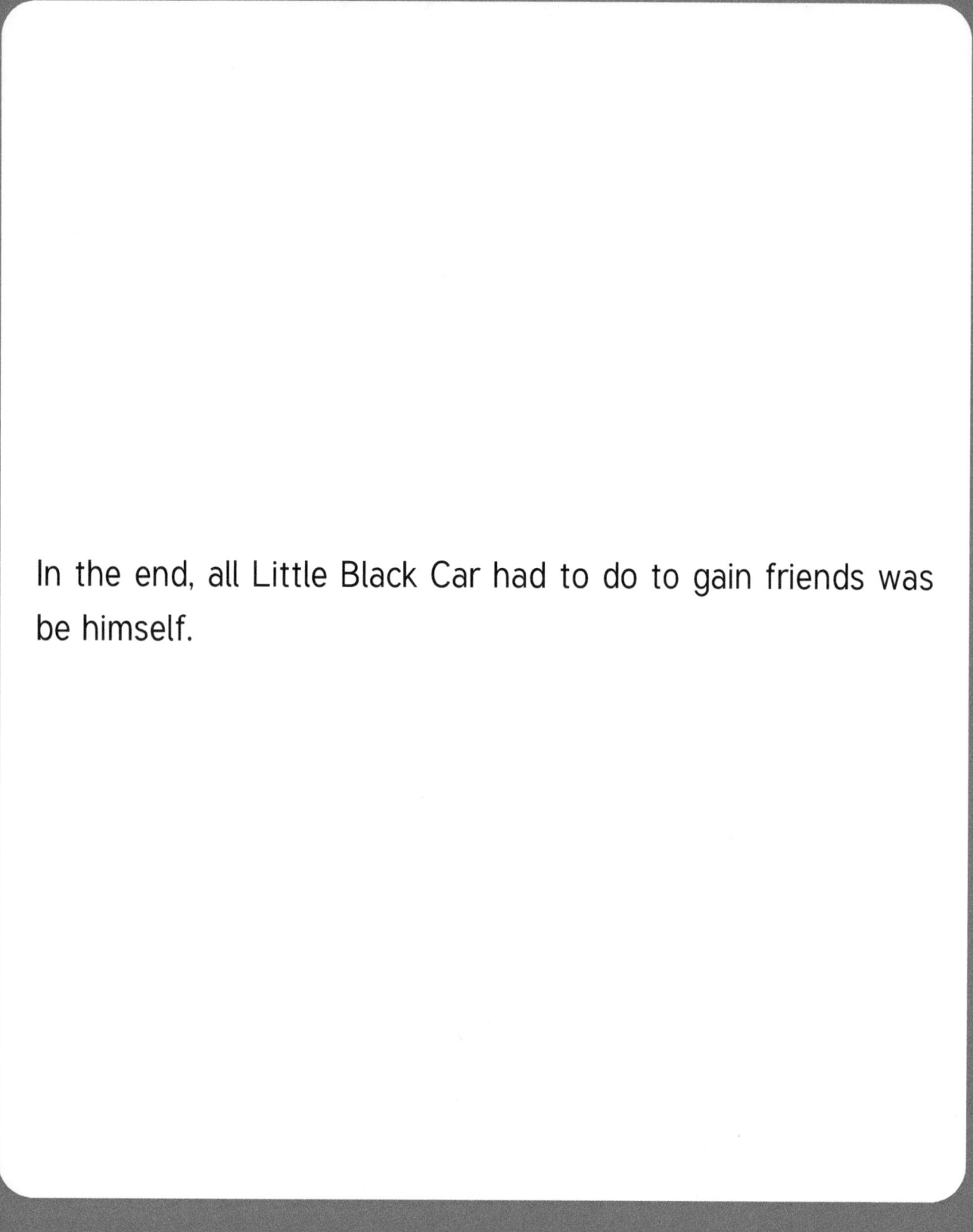

In the end, all Little Black Car had to do to gain friends was be himself.

About the Author

Imani Diop is a holistic health-care provider who also authors books. She was inspired by her son, Xavier, to write *Little Black Car*. Her efforts at character building and creating themes of unity are small steps to increasing friendships and helping young children grow to be adults who have successful relationships. A resident of Florida, she also wishes to make sunshine infectious while increasing love and laughter everywhere.

CPSIA information can be obtained
at www.ICGtesting.com
Printed in the USA
BVHW020146200821
614790BV00008B/58